Poems Of Life And Love

Emily M. Eronico

Ukiyoto Publishing

All global publishing rights are held by

Ukiyoto Publishing

Published in 2023

Content Copyright © Emily M. Eronico

ISBN 9789360164355

All rights reserved.
No part of this publication may be reproduced, transmitted, or stored in a retrieval system, in any form by any means, electronic, mechanical, photocopying, recording or otherwise, without the prior permission of the publisher.

The moral rights of the author have been asserted.

This is a work of fiction. Names, characters, businesses, places, events, locales, and incidents are either the products of the author's imagination or used in a fictitious manner. Any resemblance to actual persons, living or dead, or actual events is purely coincidental.

This book is sold subject to the condition that it shall not by way of trade or otherwise, be lent, resold, hired out or otherwise circulated, without the publisher's prior consent, in any form of binding or cover other than that in which it is published.

www.ukiyoto.com

Dedication

This book is dedicated to all people who matters the most. Your presence made this book totally meaningful. To all the people who are experiencing the total meaning of life that creates love. This book is all for you.

Synopsis

These poems talk about a story of life and love.

A life between struggle and hope, that came from misfortune and brokenness, in which gives hope for a betterment found in determination and success.

A love that has been showed by a mother to her so called family, that has been an essential part of their lives. A love created by brokenness and nothingness comparable enough to make augmentation of happiness even to each contradictory condition. So much love to express that shows no room for hate and revenge. And an impossible dream that focuses on having fantasy over reality. These poems make people realized the essence of their daily living towards a better world.

Contents

Woman	1
Love	2
Hero	3
She	5
Respect	6
Flowers Of Love	8
She Is A Woman	10
Past Of Her	13
Life	15
Measures Of Love	16
A Love To Last	17
The Clock	26
Justice	28
Madness	30
In Contrast	31
Hope	33
Irony Of Love	35
An Angels	37
About the Author	*39*

Woman

Today, I've found a woman.
As old as yesteryears
A one that has been created to have a life.
And through her life she gave life's too
Nothing to be compared of
In this place totally called world
In times of hardship she will never surrender
Beyond the odds of time, she always stays.
To fulfill her undying duty not only for herself
But meaningfully in those that belongs to her.
Those lives that originally breathed into her being
Call her a lady, down to this rushing world!
Alas! It has so untiringly made her not rest.
For even when she slept, she is always called mom.
Woman she become that is so much wonderful.
That knows no limits beyond her unrestfulness.
Time doesn't pass her boundary.
Enough to be able to have her own.
She spent no time on herself.
Coz her given life belongs not only to her,
As a woman that devotedly gave her best
To those that she loves the most.

- -

Love

Love! ironically spells the word woman.
How wondrous would it be,
To feel that there's nothing as precious as it is
Under the innate being of the so-called mother
That comes from her innermost heart.
Suffice yet unlimitedly wrapped;
Tenderly, gently, and lovingly into her soft caring arms
Embraced by her unending protection.
No one would dare to have the most affection,
Down the road that needs attention
Only a mother could truly have intention.
She keeps moving into her direction.
Towards the lane with determination
Capturing moments full of admiration
How sweetly she became a woman of no negotiation.
No amount of definition
Could describes her motivation.
Into her path of no return
How she can handle motherhood
That is found into her innermost heart.
Totally called Love.!

Hero

There could be no hero without an extreme power.
A one that made them known and famous
Over their supernaturality
Defines their outmost strength.
That cover up all the happenings
Where there is a need of help wherein,
A hero's essence is in presence, thus;
I found that hero in this living place.
We call her woman not in disguise
Her being one of a kind,
Derived her to be a kind of a hero;
That surpasses the battles of time.
Thrown by the ups and downs motion of this rolling world.
She figured things positively,
Despite the uncertainty
She keeps moving.
Under her fighting spirit
Unfold the untold history.
Where hopes demand no failure
Around this evolving era
Of no ending history
A place to where woman,
Evolved packed with never ending strength.

That a mother could ever had
In this challenging world
She is the newfound hero.
That truly defines her as a woman, called mom.

She

I love the word of she
In her I found goodness
An act of genuinely
Works of a woman called she
Her flaws captured by her unfaded beauty.
That shows her untiring acceptance,
Of things found in love
Her being took her smiling face.
Of fixed emotions drowned by fate
A fate that brought her to be called mother.
Enough and as equally as a lady of
Beauty beyond responsibility
That holds her womanhood,
Into a place that is full of joys and sorrows
Trials and challenges normally cannot defeat her.
To struggle and fight towards betterness.
Wherein she strives for the name of love.
As lovely as the word she, totally found in her being;
To be the best woman called mother.

Respect

Respect! do you know what it means?
How funny, in this gen that is full of trends.
It would be a word of no meaning.
Found in the unknown world.
Scattered over the place,
Rotten with no definite act
To be followed by its descendants,
Saying hello to its future,
Back in time, where it belongs,
It bids goodbye!
But! Wait,
I've seen someone picked it up.
Oh, how courteously she holds it.
With full of cares, she slowly put it,
In a place enough to be seen
By fellows of the world
Young enough to capture its total presence.
In this undeniably innovatively
Surpassing world, where people pass by.
I figured the word she, who patiently picked the word,
Where respect is notably found
I wonder who she is?
But at last, I certainly have an answer,

To the one that is called she
A woman whom I called mother.
In this socially evolving world
Mother I know it is you,
Letting the world imitate
That word of no meaning
In this living place
I know there could be,
A larger space of tomorrow
Holding and following the word respect
To which I truly found in you.

Flowers Of Love

Colors of hopes
Fragrance of sweetness
Aroma of love
Shows the beauty,
Of its lovely flowers.
If flowers could be a human
How lovely could it be.
To simply share its happiness
Around the world desperately unable
To value the true meaning of love
If flowers can be a human
I know it could truly give,
The hopes of never fading sweetness
That shows the meaning of care.
But they are just only flowers.
That signifies the beauty,
Found in humans, thus:
To the human I humbly dedicate those flowers
I imagined how strongly your love could,
As far as it could travelled, around the corners,
Of your four cornered heart that flows
The never-ending love,
Of a majestically endeavor, that defines your unending field.

Such lovely word in the name of a mother

I know it much be happier to have such flowers.

As far as it could offer the true definition of my truest meaning of love.

That, that flower totally defines, how I meanly called it the flowers of love.!

She Is A Woman

She; as what they say as her

A lady perfectly called woman.

Strong and innovative one

Commonly active and ready for every changed.

She is kind and a concrete reciprocal of love!

No matter what she does, it always contribute to a meaning of a word success

She might be a part of a failure,

Where she acted like a demure

Still, she's a lady, with dignity.

Sometimes she is weak.

For you to have a trick

But when she is over

Courage brought her power.

Never underestimate her beauty

To let things under her shoulders

The moment she cries, tears make her tougher

A girl in general

Denotes no material,

Upon her aching heart

That could take her apart.

So, call her a woman.

As brave as a man,

Despite her inability
No wonder how she cares.
For it is one of her duties,
To make a wondrous place
Under the spell, that no one needs to hear.
Sometimes she could be dangerous,
But nobody calls her notorious
Coz, a lady could do no harm.
Just call her vicious,
Oftentimes derived by an abused
Lady, there could be no definite words
How woman can make no excuses
Beneath the unsaid battles
That needs more struggle.
Just bear in her mind
How damaged not to rewind.
Simply put in her heart
A love pure and warm
Where she could create a space
Enough to feel happiness
That could not be replaced,
By any treat and trick
Just call her a woman
Beyond no deception
Under your gimmick
In any kind of human
A lady only needs protection.

For she is also fragile

That sounds so quiet.

Her face full of smile

Cannot forgot violence.

That's full of sorrows and miseries.

So, while she's still young,

Motivation moves her to unpacked.

All her hurtful feelings

For when she will be old enough

She could handle things over her strength.

Gentle yet amazing , lady could be so high

Towards what makes her as purposeful as she is

Worthy to be crowned as a lady as equally called woman.

Past Of Her

Changeable and able
That's who she is.
Yesteryears she was but a lady perfect for recreation.
But today, I found her mingling household chores
Yesteryears she had freedom of no worries.
Now is for her, the times of many anxieties,
Worry, she used not to feel!
Oh! Woman as she is; there could be no reason,
Why she cannot feel the feeling of unworriness,
Under a mother's instinct of perspective!
Of today's unsafe condition.
Yesteryears she devotes her time alone for herself.
How can she do that for a moment?
When her times cannot suffice the duties
That times offer most dearly.
I figured her happiness found in her past.
Totally different from that of today.
A woman as always being called,
Is now a name calling found in yesteryears.
For today, it is her passion to be normally called mother.
Eager to see the future that belongs to her children.
That was never to be imagined as far as it was before,
Truly her only intention is to be able to live happily.

Together now and ever being with her family
Those past that she had were only a living memories ended as part
Of her truly amazing life story
For she is now a fully fulfilled woman, in the name of a mother.

Life

   Life, how wonderful
   Full of surprises
    Subject for any change
  If it could only be a river
How could it be so strong?
For waters to flow as fast as it could
If life could be called heaven
It will be so much a delight.
Knowing how perfect heaven it could be.
If life could be a music
Then it could be always that bright
No amount of sorrows could never be that light.
For in music there is total chances to dance with the flow.
But the truth is, it is called life, a mother could give.
Sharing the greatest blessing, life is the only name.
If life could be a matter to exchange
It simply says its always be the same being that living piece
For in life, no exact word could truly be called if
For in life all the if, could have it all!
Dear mother, saying thank you is never enough,
To cherish the most blessing found in life.!

Measures Of Love

You are but a masterpiece.

Puzzles of chances

Brought by heaven down to earth.

Like stars that is up above

That lights the darkest path,

Like the sun whose brightness never cease

Like the moon that never overpasses

The absence of the reigning sun over the day.

Like the water that truly indicates the significance of life

Like the flowers that comfort the shadow of the grievest soul

Like the ocean that gives the true meaning of uncertainty

If love could be totally measures out of these

Then there could be no reason to take the part of it.

Like the mountains that is possibly one of the hardest ways to achieve

The demand of this so called love never compromises to a mother dearest care

Upon her growing children, that withstand the changes of each passing time.

Down to the road of never-ending story that life and love withholds.

A Love To Last

I never knew what love is.
Tell I found you,
My world is lonely without you.
Till I met you,
That makes my world lovely.
Being with you makes me happy,
That makes my complete day.
Yesterday was sadness.
But today is full of gladness.
Yesterday was a make belief that,
I'm a dreamer to make a wish.
That one day, someone can feel to miss,
To someone like me.
Now that it's already true,
My heart will never be in blue.
That directs my notion.
That my love is truly in great motion.
If tomorrow would be a dream,
I hope it would not be a lame.
That might bring my love to vain.
That unable to walk and stand the pain,
For today, my love, honey makes me strong.
Thus, cannot be so wrong.

I figure that you and I
Will commit that love to last.
A love that never had a past,
To make the story long.
For, you and I will stay.
That must be so great.
When I glance that tomorrow,
I guess it will not have to borrow.
The time that I spent waiting!
My life that's starts complaining.
How miserable a life that has no one claiming,
To my heart that is so loving.
That I really start giving,
Till I meet you, darling.
You are the star that keeps shining.
To my path, I keep walking.
As I look with you.
My heart keeps beating,
I know it will not stop taking,
The courage to continue making.
That wondrous moment of caring,
To someone like you, my love.
That precious gift I had
Will never make me mad.
To have you my lad,
Soon to be called a dad.

When I remembered yesterday,
It was so funny,
Reminding my gloomy days
Nothing without you,
It was just an ordinary moment.
Complying simple event.
For a dreamer to take
A love to make.
Now that we're here.
Sharing the same feeling,
I demand nothing.
But a heart that is so loving,
Giving me the strength to still hoping
That our love will be more in keeping
The most unbearable thing,
That will someday make us longing.
To have our love admiring
That power that keeps us striving
To never had our love an ending.

That's the very desire of my heart.
To never had a moment to hurt.
That will start bleeding,
In the most inner part, it keeps digging.
Till it will soon be breaking
That I don't really want crying
So please darling, help me saving.

That true love I had with you letting,
Be a continues process of believing.
That it totally last until forever.

But my love I know that it's only a fantasy.
That keeps my mind turning.
Letting myself fearing
Of things that will never be happening
That someday you will be going.
To make our story a living
Part of the untold history.

 For I know, how great your love for me is.
I see that heart of you untiringly,
Able to stay beyond the warning.
Of the challenging battles of the captivating,
Enticing eyes of the deceiver.
Yet, my beloved you are truly amazing.
For letting yourself standing,
In the aisle where your holding
The covenant of your purely loving heart
Where I'm happily looking
The very loyal one I'm keeping.

Time will let us know.
How we keep on trying
To have a much faithful vow

Between our unaffected devotion
That leads to our strong emotion.
Of both undeniable affection
That tells the world our appreciation.
Of how it belongs to our addiction.
That loving us becomes an obsession
To never had a problem to be of solution.
Till it falls under negotiation.
That never had a time of resolution.

I know till our life is filling,
The current situation it is having.
Our love will continue fulfilling.
The moment of love it is committing.
Between our individual indifference
There is no one to make nonsense.
To depart us simply by having excuses
For I know we have embraces
The uncertainty of time that messes
Nothing but how we interface.
Of such underlying circumstances.

Being with you in time
Will make my life align.
In the so-called agony
I'm going to be so fine,
For I never had a time

Making it be mine.

I treasure moments lastingly.
Having you with me
For having you makes me honestly,
The very lucky one
That I'm truly thankful with
For you're the one I'm relying on
In making my life meaningful one.

So, to you my one and only love
Hold my hands, never let me go.
Time will be our teller.
Never our breaker
To let us live together,
Till forever.

My heart dictates rarely
To you I stand bravely
To lasts our love strongly.
Letting it continually
Living happily.

When sorrows arrive
Depriving our happiness
Let us be more entice,
Figuring love alive

That it will be suffice
In line with togetherness.

Problems can be solved.
Never be at risk.
Taking it alone
For me and you are here
Surviving our faith
That nothing can't be unsolved.

It is not just between love.
To cherish our hopes
That demands only us.
To uphold the story of love
That stands between us.
Yet, it is also how strong our foundation would be.
To untangle the undesirable that has in us.
So, I humbly ask you darling.
Be my only living,
Hero of surviving
To let surpassing.
The highly unbearable,
Only by feeling,
Of unending loving
Between us, oh! Sweet darling.

Money would be a matter.

But don't be bothered.
Coz, it is just a thing,
Nothing to be distressed.
It is something out to be concerned.
For it is just quiet materially created
For us to be breathing,
Indeed, love between us never to be disturbed.
For us to be failed.
Know darling, how faithful,
My love it is beautiful.
So, let us be more prayerful.
For us to be humble
When we are going to stumble
Let us be gentle.
Being more delightful
In the midst in this horrible time
Let us be more acceptable.
Able to handle,
Every undesirable
Impact of time.

Let us be a living witness.
To tell the world
That having our love,
Would be the greatest,
Blessing we ever received.
Till our love lasts

Till forever
Even until eternity
That defines infinity.
 A love to last forever!

- Emily M. Eronico

The Clock

Tiktak! tiktak! Round says the clock.
Tiktak! tiktak! The one that tells the hours.
Tiktak! Tiktak! That was hastily chaste by ours.
Tiktak! Tiktak! A time no to waste
For every single minute, needs not to wait.
For time is as precious as gold
So, there's no time for you to hold.
For every drop of its hand
The clock, wants to utter to say goodbye
Down to its journey, that it only had
Into a world that has no land
Till you find yourself joining its busy hands.
To make a round, till it's gone.
Like ashes that vanished in the air
Simply when the wind blows, that makes the dust.
How funny to say that there's no one in the world.
Could literally stop the ticking of the clock.
Till it's literally broken, magically stops.
How impressive to that very hands, that created,
The busiest thing on earth
That never stops turning, till the world finds its rest.
So, why do you hesitate?
Not to follow the ticking of the clock?

Very akin to myself, wasting moment,
As if it could be regained.
Forgot not to hold the time.
Just to save, the never ending lost
Of an unforgettable segment,
Of our everyday life
Taking back the golden episode
Of an untiring ticking of the clock
Takes no chances to behold.
So while there's still a little time
Make a round and follow the clock.
Its restless hands that work persistently
Is so shameful on our part, to ignore;
How lifeless could act to do some more.
As fast as if it took no past.
So, folk be like as what the clock is,
Continuously able to do our best.
Despite our unstoppable story of ups and down
There could be a clock that says,
Tiktak! tiktak! To remind us of our every life's
Most unforgettable story.
So be with the clock till it stops turning!

Justice

You took a name.
That has no fame,
Never! forever!
You took a sight.
Without a flight
Morning till its night
You look so good,
But has no mood.
Sorry tells its hood.
So, where's the pen?
It looks like pale,
She writes for all men.
Down stands a male.
Where you go, I feel so sure,
Its likely not so pure
So, have a look.
And talk some more.
What happens when it shook?
 You said you shot.
And take the plot,
Hurt feels a lot.
So, men keep saying.
Hard no more playing,

Life's full of please
Begging is not easy.
 You are just longing.
Not for belonging,
Whom are you in?
Without a heart within
So, please there's no more lying,
Find no more trying.
Thinking it's not flying.
For loud and clear
You are so dear,
Nothing's gonna crying,
Till it's not hurting
For all is just loving.

Madness

Hurtful yet truthful
Sorrow to borrow,
Brings no tomorrow.
Do you think it is just a game?
For no one's to be blame.
It takes so painful,
Let's just be hopeful.
That it takes no prank
That has no rank.
Let just be prayerful,
To make it beautiful
For madness is sadness
That needs more gladness.
So, tell me it's okay,
To roam around no hey!
For madness takes no play
In a world that need to pay.
Keep madness be no more,
And let it be stored,
In a place that has no shore.
So, let it had a flight,
In a place that has no fight,
Till madness has no name
In a worlds' that full of fame.

In Contrast

This is just a story,
Of a one that has no glory
Living In a life of worry
In a world full of memory
While the other is so much lucky
Gaining a lot of power
In a place that has a tower
Leading a life full of wacky,
And the other has no more angle.
In a life that has been tangle
In a place full of misery
That has no more mystery.
Where could be the one has meaning?
Without a way of giving,
Taking a life so busy
That has been so messy.
While the other set himself freely
Spending life happily
In a life pack with freedom
To have no boredom
Yet, the other gives no treasure,
In a road where there's no way
To make a better day,

It has no more pressure.

In keeping time, a dream

So, to whom do you have no pleasure?

Putting thyself in leisure

Keeping oneself alive

Meaning that needs to revive

Where there's no more in contrast

In a world that's needs to last.

Hope

She said she was in vain.
Letting things without a gain
Leading her heart in pain
She stopped, resting herself.
Watching people do their share,
Do nothing but full of shame.
What does it mean to let it go?
A hurtful episode of not knowing,
Finding someone that has no meaning.
Around she turns and sees some more.
Alas! Finding hope in another's world.
There she acted like it is her own,
Where she stays, notion to move on.
Creating a world of fantasy
Damage to repair
Love to share, dare to exist.
How to maintain, a battle to resist?
Addicted to acquiring a bundle of happiness,
Within a place where no to insist.
What's within in a world called reality?
Let it be, says the day.
For there's still tomorrow that needs to shine.
Waiting for that love to grow

Until it blooms and glow

Rejecting moments of trying

Till it stops crying

Letting things better

Till it lasts forever,

In a place that is called Hope.!

Irony Of Love

Broken and agonizing heart
Found lonely and in misery.
Keep in silent mood,
By the one who let it close.
Distance by closure
Acted like nothing's happened.
Till it rests, sorrow to bury.
In a vanishable memory
Glad it found someone to lend on.
Enveloped with joy,
Burden to overcome.
Battling with trying
Never surrender,
She opened her heart again.
Overloading happiness
Weakness to strengthen.
Love created goodness,
Entering a path of new direction
Aching and hurtful moments.
Was once a memorable episode.
Now she found a place,
Like a star in shape,
Lights that shine her heart

Formed into greater beginning,
Tomorrow is an anticipation,
Where it found its sweetest glory.

An Angels

An angels in the sky
That can so high fly
Made people look and stop.
To stare and have a glance,
On their so angelic faces
And unfamiliar appearances
Match no one on the land
Even to the very rich
That has the power to reach,
The highly unreachable
Those angels we had seen.
Not only on the sky
Will never had a chance,
To make our lives stuck
To capture the moment
Of that very rare instance
On an angel to stay
On our very own comfortable home
 called heaven on earth,
How poor to those angels
That has been sent from above,
That has never been considered special in our hearts.
We only look at them once,

But never invited them to have a stay,
They are just like an ordinary folks,
Making business out of stock.
How sweet to those angels
To comply their task
Without a rush
I wish I could be one of them,
Not to be called fellow
Of this so chaos and troubled world
Just like those angles
I wish I had a chance,
I can be so close to heaven,
That is so far away,

As earth cannot reach
I wish I could be those
angels
That can stay,
Yet has the power to leave.
That no one could normally do
As powerful and instantly
Those angels do and have.
I wish I could be one of those angels,
That has the chance to fly and look to people
Without doing harm
Yet give us calm.
I wish I could be one of those angels in the name of grace.

About the Author

Emily M. Eronico

Emily is a public school teacher for almost a decade. Solitude is one of her passion and habit. She improves herself in simple gathering as mandated in the institution where she works. Her simple passion in literature ignites her to make simple literary works.

www.ingramcontent.com/pod-product-compliance
Lightning Source LLC
LaVergne TN
LVHW041558070526
838199LV00046B/2044